Abuelita (ah-bweh-LEE-tah): Spanish for Grandma, Grandmother

Book design by Kimi Weart
Book production by The Kids at Our House
The text is set in ITC Korinna
The illustrations are rendered in pencil, then colored digitally
Manufactured in China by RR Donnelley
10 9 8 7 6 5
First Edition

Library of Congress Cataloging-in-Publication Data
Names: Newman, Lesléa, author. | Mola, Maria, illustrator.
Title: Sparkle boy / by Lesléa Newman ; illustrations by Maria Mola.
Description: First edition. | New York : Lee & Low Books Inc., [2017] |
Summary: "Three-year-old Casey wants what his older sister, Jessie, has—
a shimmery skirt, glittery painted nails, and a sparkly bracelet—but Jessie
does not approve. After two boys tease Casey about his appearance,
Jessie evolves to a place of acceptance and celebration of her
gender creative younger brother"— Provided by publisher.
Identifiers: LCCN 2016028288 | ISBN 9781620142851 (hardcover : alk. paper)
Subjects: | CYAC: Gender identity—Fiction. | Brothers and sisters—Fiction. |
Bullying—Fiction.
Classification: LCC PZ7.N47988 Sp 2017 | DDC [Fic]—dc23
LC record available at https://lccn.loc.gov/2016028288

For Sparkle Boys everywhere.
You make the world bright! —*L.N.*

For my little bright boy, Marc —*M.M.*

Jessie adored all things shimmery, glittery, and sparkly.

"Look at my shimmery skirt," Jessie said to her little brother, Casey, as she twirled into the living room and her skirt twirled out all around her.

Casey looked up from his alphabet blocks. "Ooh, shimmery, shimmery," he said, reaching out his hand. "I want shimmery."

Jessie stopped twirling, and her skirt stopped twirling too. "You can't have a shimmery skirt, Casey," she said.

"Why?" Casey asked.

"Because boys don't wear shimmery skirts," said Jessie. "Right, Mama?"

Mama thought for a minute. "If Casey wants to wear a skirt, Casey can wear a skirt," she said. "I don't have a problem with that."

Mama went upstairs and came back with a skirt that was now too small for Jessie. "Here, buddy," she said to Casey. "Try this on."

"Ooh, shimmery, shimmery!" Casey said as he twirled around and his shimmery skirt twirled out all around him. Casey twirled and twirled until he got dizzy and plopped down on his bottom. Casey laughed.

Jessie frowned.

The next afternoon Jessie went to a birthday party.
When she came home, she raced into the kitchen.
"Look at my glittery nails," Jessie said, fanning out
her fingers. Her nails glittered in the light.

Casey looked up from his animal puzzle. "Ooh, glittery, glittery," he said, pulling Jessie's hands toward him. "I want glittery."

Jessie snatched her hands away. "You can't have glittery nails, Casey," she said.

"Why?" Casey asked.

"Because boys don't wear glittery nail polish," said Jessie. "Right, Daddy?"

Daddy thought for a minute. "Most boys don't wear nail polish," he said. "But Casey can if he wants to. There's no harm in that."

Daddy went upstairs and came back with a bottle of glittery polish.

"Can't you just paint his toenails?" Jessie asked. "And then make him put on his socks?"

"That's not a bad idea," Daddy said to Casey. "What do you say, pal?"

"No!" Casey shouted. He held out his hands and kept them perfectly still while Daddy painted his fingernails.

"Ooh, glittery, glittery!" Casey said as he spread his fingers wide so his nails glittered in the light.

Jessie shook her head.

The next morning Jessie and Casey's grandmother came to visit.

"Abuelita, I like your sparkly bracelets," said Jessie.

"You can have one. I have plenty," Abuelita said. She took off a bracelet and slid it onto Jessie's wrist. Jessie swiveled her arm back and forth and watched the bracelet sparkle.

Casey looked up from his dump truck. "Ooh, sparkly, sparkly," Casey said. "I want sparkly."

Jessie hid her arm behind her back. "You can't have a sparkly bracelet, Casey," she said.

"Why?" Casey asked.

"Because boys don't wear sparkly bracelets," said Jessie. "Right, Abuelita?"

Abuelita thought for a minute. "I've never seen a boy wear a sparkly bracelet . . . ," she said,

". . . until now."

Abuelita turned to Casey. "Here, Sparkle Boy," she said. She took off another bracelet and slid it onto Casey's arm. "There's no reason why Casey can't wear a bracelet, Jessie. He isn't hurting anyone."

"Ooh, sparkly, sparkly!" Casey said as he swiveled his arm back and forth and watched his bracelet sparkle.

Jessie stomped her foot and ran inside.

On Saturday Daddy went grocery shopping, and Mama
took Jessie and Casey to the library.

Jessie came downstairs wearing her shimmery skirt and
sparkly bracelet. Her nails glittered in the light.

Soon Mama came downstairs with Casey. He wore his
shimmery skirt and his sparkly bracelet. His nails glittered
in the light too.

"Mama!" Jessie cried as she thrust her fists onto her hips.
"Why is Casey dressed like that?"

"Because that's how Casey wants to dress," Mama said.

"But that's not how boys are supposed to dress," said
Jessie. "Casey looks silly."

"I don't think Casey looks silly," Mama said, smiling at
him. "I think Casey looks like Casey."

When Jessie, Casey, and Mama got to the library, story time had already started. They sat in the back to listen. After the librarian finished reading, Mama went to the front desk to check out some books. Jessie and Casey waited for her in the children's room.

"I like your skirt," a girl said to Jessie. "And I like your sister's skirt."

Jessie didn't say anything.

"I'm not a sister," Casey said. "I'm a brother."

"You can't be a brother," said the girl.

"Why?" asked Casey.

"Because you're a girl," she answered.

"I'm a boy," said Casey.

"You are?" an older boy said. He stared at Casey and then laughed. "Hey, look," he called to his friend. "A boy in a skirt."

The boy's friend laughed too. Then he knelt in front of Casey. "Dude," he said. "You can't go around wearing a skirt."

"Why?" Casey asked.

"Because you look weird, and everyone will laugh at you," said the boy.

"Why?" Casey asked again.

"Because boys don't wear skirts and bracelets and nail polish. Everybody knows that," said the boy. "Right?" he asked, turning to Jessie.

Jessie looked at Casey. His face was scrunching up like it always did right before he started to cry.

"Why can't boys wear skirts and bracelets and nail polish?" Jessie asked the boys.

"Because," said one of the boys.

"That's just the way it is," said the other.

"Not anymore," said Jessie as she put her arm around Casey's shoulder. "Come on, little guy," she said. "Let's find Mama and go home."

Jessie and Casey adored all things
shimmery, glittery, and sparkly, . . .